For Lyn Oates, who has seen a golden hare.
For Cathy Cooper and a piece of synchronicity.
For Nicola Davies who suggested 'silver'.
For all the singers, and most of all for the innocent hare.

JANETTA OTTER-BARRY BOOKS

Song of the Golden Hare copyright © Frances Lincoln Limited 2013
Text and illustrations copyright © Jackie Morris 2013
First published in Great Britain and in the USA in 2013 by
Frances Lincoln Children's Books,
74-77 White Lion Street, London N1 9PF
www.franceslincoln.com

A catalogue record for this book is available from the British Library.

ISBN 978-1-84780-450-1

Illustrated with Windsor & Newton artist's quality watercolours, on Arches hotpress watercolour paper

Set in Cochin

Printed and bound in China

1 3 5 7 9 8 6 4 2

Song of the Golden Hare

Jackie Morris

F

FRANCES LINCOLN
CHILDREN'S BOOKS

The boy loved hares for their twilight dancing
wildness, the light in their amber eyes, their long
velvet ears, their speed.

And he loved music for the way it made his heart
dance inside him. He often played, strumming
and plucking delicate tunes on his harp.

But he never sang. For some reason
he thought he couldn't.

He had always known that his family
was special. While others in the village
would hunt the hares with fierce, swift
hounds, his grandfather would seek out
orphaned leverets, raise them until
they were strong and then set them free,
back into the wild land.

"You never know," he would say,
"which might be 'the one'."

But this wasn't why the family was special.
It was because they held the secret of
the golden hare, and they held it very close.

Once, every fifty years or so, all the hares
in the land would gather together.
In a clearing in the woods, the males
would strive to win the heart of
the Golden Queen of the Hares –
for a new queen was needed.

A few people, who had heard rumours
of golden hares, thought this was
why hares boxed in the twilight.
But the family knew that the hares
would sing, and this was how
one hare would win the queen's heart.

It was the task of the boy's family to keep the old queen safe, to make sure that at the end of her days she reached the shore and crossed to the Island of the Golden Hares.

For others who had heard of the golden hare thought to catch and kill her, sure that her golden coat would bring wealth and health to whoever possessed it.

And how the boy ached to hear the hares sing. No one knew when it would happen. His mother had lived her life without a whisper of hare-song.

Grandfather often sang strange
soft melodies when he tended
the orphans, gentle music as the
tiny creatures rested, warm in
the bowl of his huge hands.
The boy would try to catch these
melodies in the strings of his harp,
weaving the tune with his clever
fingers while Grandfather
hummed and sang.

And then one day the hares
began to move.

The boy was awake early, out in the twilight
dew-dropped morning. At first one, then two,
then more and more hares began to move across
the land from east to west, shadows made long
by low morning sunlight.

He ran home, woke his sister
and they gathered together food,
a blanket, a flask for water.
And away they ran, hand in hand,
following the hares, leaving behind
two sleeping people and a note:
"We are gone, for the hares are running."

They followed. Over the hills, across streams, through forests, bridging rivers, moving in the twilight darkness, fearful of hound, hawk and huntsman. The hares knew that the two children followed them, and they knew who they were.

But someone else followed the children, hiding, secret. He had heard of the Queen of the Hares and in his greed he thought he would get a very fine price for her golden fur.

They came at last to an ancient wood of twisted oak,
hard by the sea. In the wood a wide clearing began
to fill with brown hares and white mountain hares,
and on a raised mound in the middle, on a moon-white rock,
sat the most beautiful creature the boy had ever seen.
Silence fell.

It seemed to the children that the world stood still
and listened. One by one the hares stepped forward
to sing, and oh, but they had never heard such
music before.

On the edge of the clearing the boy stood with his sister
and watched and listened. And he thought his heart
would break with the beauty of each wild song.

He listened with his ears and he listened with his heart
and he longed to find each song in the strings of his harp.
And that was when he realised he had left it
behind at home.

Just when he thought that the hare-song
could not be more beautiful,
one last hare came forward to sing.

Small and ragged of ear, a vagabond runt of a creature –
and yet the children recognised the hare,
for this was one that their grandfather had raised.

From the very first note they knew that their hare
had won the queen's heart.

As the hare's song ended
there was a texture to
the silence held in every leaf
of every tree
in the wild wood.

Then, one by one, the hares
began to drift away
through the gathering
darkness.

Moths took to the air.
Only the queen
and the vagabond,
the boy and his sister
remained.

The summer began to wear away as the boy and his sister
watched over the pair. The nights brought a chill.
Mornings brought a frosting to the grass.

The hare and his bride had a beautiful golden
leveret child, bright as the first star of morning,
in a nest of silvered grass.

She grew fast. Foxes barked in the wild wood.
But the children kept watch and the hares were safe.

One morning the old queen came to the children
in the early hours. It was time for her to leave.
And so they began the short journey away from
the shelter of the wild wood and towards the shore.

This was the time of greatest danger. A new queen
in the wild wood and the old queen, worn and tired.
If she could reach the shore, and cross the wide space
of the sea, she would be safe forever on the
Island of the Golden Hares. No man could set
foot there.

High on the hill two hounds, one silver, one black,
raised their heads to read the wind and caught
the scent of gold.

Sometimes she walked beside them,
sometimes the boy carried her, tucked
warm in his jacket, next to his heart.

At first he thought it was the rhythm
of the queen's fast-beating heart that he felt
rather than heard. As the sound grew louder
he thought it was his own heart –
but then it was joined by another.

And now he knew what it was,
for he could see them, black and silver,
hounds' feet pounding the earth
as they came for her.

Swift and young were the hounds and the queen
was exhausted, the children full of fear.
The hunter sounded his horn and a blood note
ripped the air.........

Now the children, brave and still,
began to sing. At first only his sister,
a high wild note, free as a lark. Then the boy,
joining his voice for the first time with hers,
weaving and winding the hares' speed
and the twilight dancing with the threaded
memory of the hares' music, and fear and love
and beauty.

They sang until their song brought the hounds
to a halt and the huntsman to his knees.

As the children sang, the old queen began to swim
across the sea to the distant shore. She faltered
mid-stream, so tired. It seemed she would
be taken by the waves.

But the children watched as a seal swam up
beneath her and lifted her light across the water.
In the setting sun it seemed that the seal was golden,
not grey.

The distant island glowed for a while as if the sun itself
was setting there. As darkness fell it disappeared,
perhaps for another fifty years.

The children fell silent. Hand in hand, they turned
away from the sea and began the long walk home,
two great hounds at their heels, one silver, one black.
For a while the soft voice of the wild seal followed them.

It is said that, now and again, if your heart is good,
as the sun sets, you might catch sight of a golden island
resting on the sea's edge. If you are really lucky
you might hear a faint trace of music, hare-song,
mingling with the sound of the waves.

If you are really lucky.